The illustrations for this book were drawn and colored in Procreate.

Cataloging-in-Publication Data has been applied for and may be obtained from the Library of Congress.

ISBN 978-1-4197-5191-2

Text and illustrations © 2022 Drew Brockington
Book design by Jade Rector

Printed and bound in China
10 9 8 7 6 5 4 3 2 1

Abrams Books for Young Readers are available at special discounts when purchased in quantity for premiums and promotions as well as fundraising or educational use. Special editions can also be created to specification. For details, contact specialsales@abramsbooks.com or the address below.

Abrams® is a registered trademark of Harry N. Abrams, Inc.

ABRAMS The Art of Books
195 Broadway, New York, NY 10007
abramsbooks.com

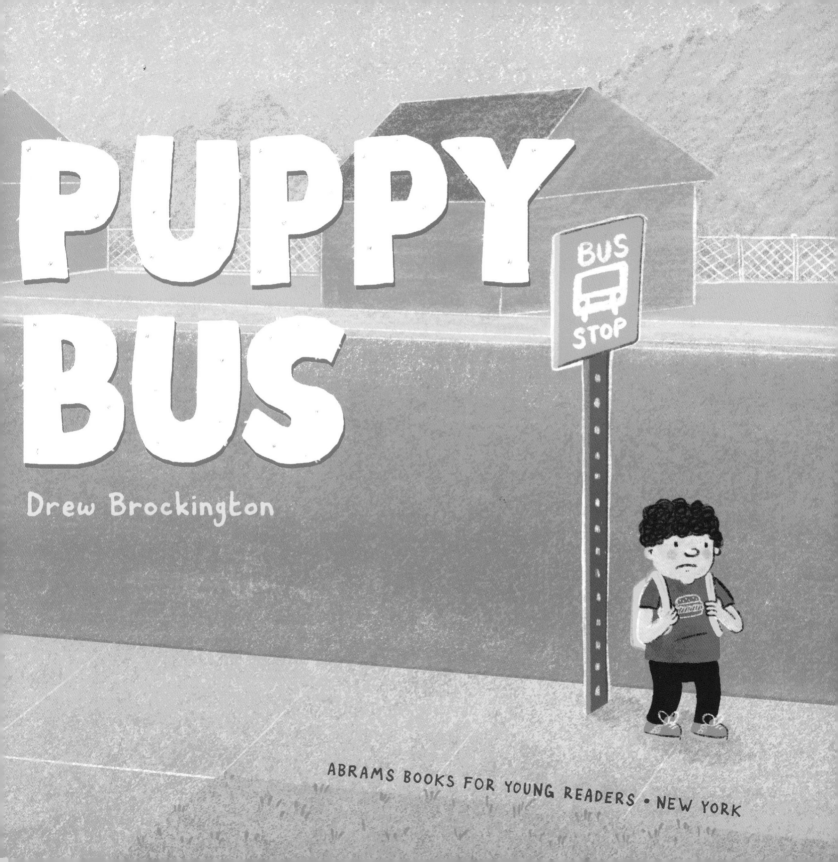

PUPPY
BUS

Drew Brockington

ABRAMS BOOKS FOR YOUNG READERS • NEW YORK

Who's got two thumbs and is ready for the first day at a new school?

The teachers will be different.

I'll have to make all new friends.

I won't even know where the bathroom is.

This is the worst.

What is this place?

Do I have to go to school here?

Where is everyone?

I should find a grown-up
and tell them what's happened.

Everything about this school
is strange and different.

The subjects don't make sense.

Lunch looks disgusting.

And the bathroom is VERY confusing.

Things are looking pretty glum.

I miss my old school.

I miss my friends.

I want to go home.

There are balls to throw!

Grass for running
and jumping!

Dirt for digging!

There's even a
bathroom outside?!

I could get used to this.

Maybe this school isn't so bad after all.

Who's got two paws and is excited for the second day of school?